CLEAN YOUR ROOM, HARVEY MOON!

YOUR ROOM, HARVEY MOON!

by Pat Cummings

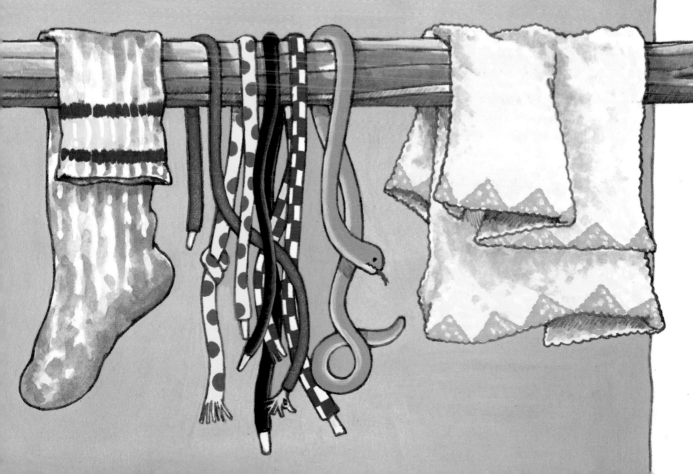

Aladdin Paperbacks
An imprint of Simon & Schuster
Children's Publishing Division
1230 Avenue of the Americas
New York, NY 10020
Copyright © 1991 by Pat Cummings
All rights reserved including the right of reproduction
in whole or in part in any form.
First Aladdin Paperbacks edition, 1994
Manufactured in China
21 22
The text of this book is set in 16 point Windsor O.S. Light.
About the illustrations: An underdrawing in line was rendered in ink and
painted with transparent watercolors and gouache.
Book design by Pat Cummings
Typography by Julie Quan and Christy Hale

Library of Congress Cataloging-in-Publication Data
Cummings, Pat.
     Clean your room, Harvey Moon! / by Pat Cummings.—1st Aladdin
Books ed.
          p.   cm.
     Summary: Harvey tackles a big job: cleaning his room.
     ISBN 978-0-689-71798-7
     [1. Orderliness—Fiction.   2. Cleanliness—Fiction.   3. Afro-Americans—
Fiction.   4. Stories in rhyme.]   I. Title.
[PZ8.3.C898C1   1994]
[E]—dc20   93-20571

For Kali

On Saturday morning at ten to nine
Harvey Moon was eating toast,
Waiting for the cartoon show
That he enjoyed the most

With only minutes left to go,
He heard the voice of DOOM.
"Today, young man," his mother said,
"Is the day you clean your room!"

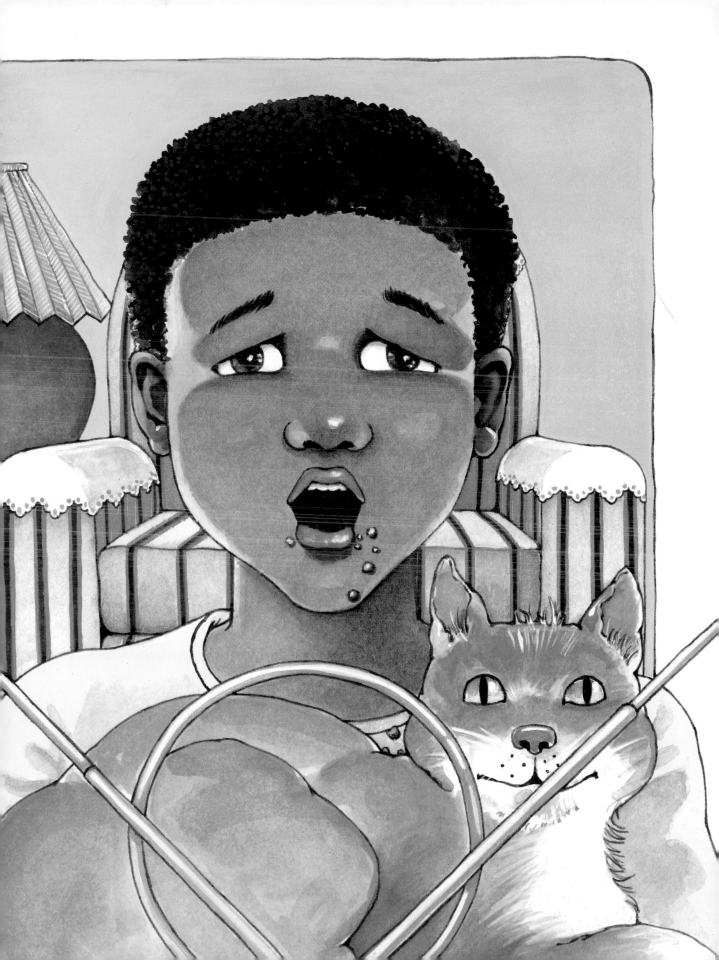

"Not nowwww…" moaned Harvey,
Red in the face.
"I'll miss 'Rotten Ed'
And 'Invaders from Space'!"
"Right this second!" she ordered,
And gave him the broom.
Harvey marched angrily
Up to his room.

It really didn't seem
Messy at all.
First he'd throw his dirty clothes
Out in the hall.
Under the bed was
An ice cream-smeared shirt,
Jeans that had what Mom called
"Ground-in dirt...."

Two towels and swim trunks
That seemed to be wet,
Three socks he sniffed
And found weren't dirty yet.
Under the dresser was a lump
Warm and gray,
That he didn't recognize
So he put it away.

The floor of the closet had clumps
Hard and dirty
Of T-shirts and sweatshirts....
IT WAS TEN-THIRTY!
Harvey panicked then thought,
"I should be through soon,
I'll eat lunch while I watch
'Creature Zero' at noon."

Grabbing marbles and crayons and
Flat bottle caps,
Two of his own special
Lightning bug traps,
The softball he couldn't find
Last Saturday,
One toothbrush, one helmet…
He put them away.

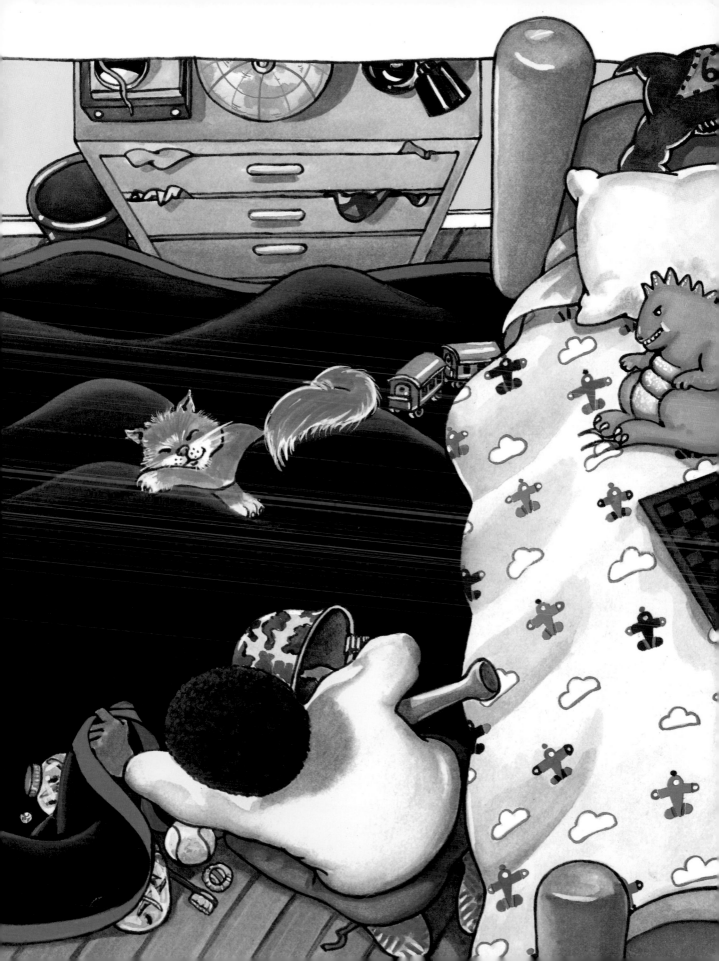

"I'll clear out these toys
And then I'll be done,
'Ken's Kung Fu Korner'
Will be on at one...."
Under his desk were some comics
All icky
From something inside
That was dripping and sticky.

He found library books
He'd forgotten he had,
His skates from Aunt Sarah,
His bow tie from dad,
He found a caboose
That was missing its train,
A whistle, paintbrushes,
A map of the brain.

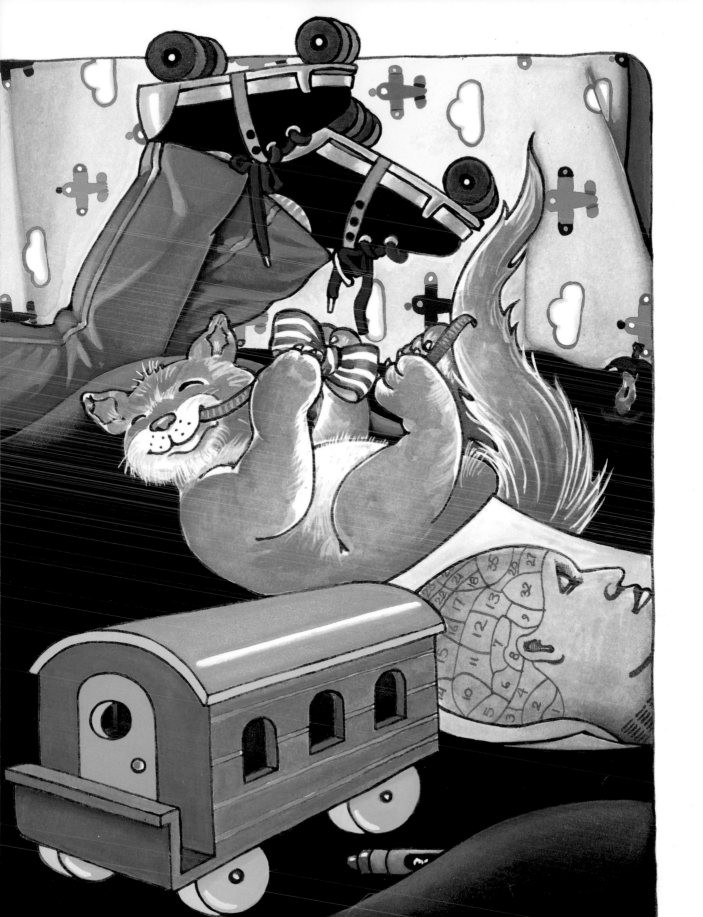

He found sneakers and card games
Up under the bed,
Goggles, flippers, and a grasshopper
...dead,
A long-lost cookie
All fuzzy and gray,
Plastic cars, boats, and planes,
And he put them away.

Just then Harvey happened
To notice the clock.
"IT'S ALMOST TWO!!" Harvey shouted.
He went into shock.
"I missed 'Caveman Capers'
On channel nine....
I'm starving! I'm tired!
This room looks fine!"

He put up his bathrobe,
His bat, and football,
With a few other things
Then ran down the hall,
Shouting, "Mom, I'm finished!"
Harvey put back the broom.
His mother stepped cautiously
Into his room.

"I'm really amazed," his mom said.
Harvey beamed.
He could watch TV now. He was through,
So it seemed.
"I fixed you some lunch," she said.
"When you are done,
You and I will get started
On lump number one!"

THE END?